LOVE-A-BULL

KATIE CHANDLER

Concept Illustrator Hannah Weitlauf

BEYOND
PUBLISHING

New York | Los Angeles | London | Sydney

Softcover ISBN: 978-1-949873-57-3

Hardcover ISBN: 978-1-949873-02-3

"I am dedicating this book to
my Tyler, my Evie and our sweet dogs
Roxy and Tuck. Thank you for making our
family whole."

LOVE-A-BULL

KATIE CHANDLER

Concept Illustrator Hannah Weitlauf

They say our breeds are bullies
But that is just not true
We kiss
We hug
We cuddle
We love to love on you

Our favorite is our baby
She likes to cuddle too

She loves to give us belly rubs
You would love them too!

She loves our fur so soft and warm
Our kisses sweet and wet

The best day of our doggie lives
Was the day that we first met

Taking walks makes her happy
And we are right there by her side

Anything to see her smile
Our love we cannot hide

Our heads are square and bodies big
But our hearts are even bigger

We'll teach her how to fetch a ball
Or be a sandbox digger

Silly faces and singing songs
The things that make her laugh

Splashing water, blowing bubbles
We help her with her bath

At night we read a book or two
Mommy's voice so soft and sweet

We kiss her on her cheek and head
We know it helps her sleep

She's nestled quietly in her crib
Her blankets soft and wore

We never want to leave her side
So we curl up on the floor

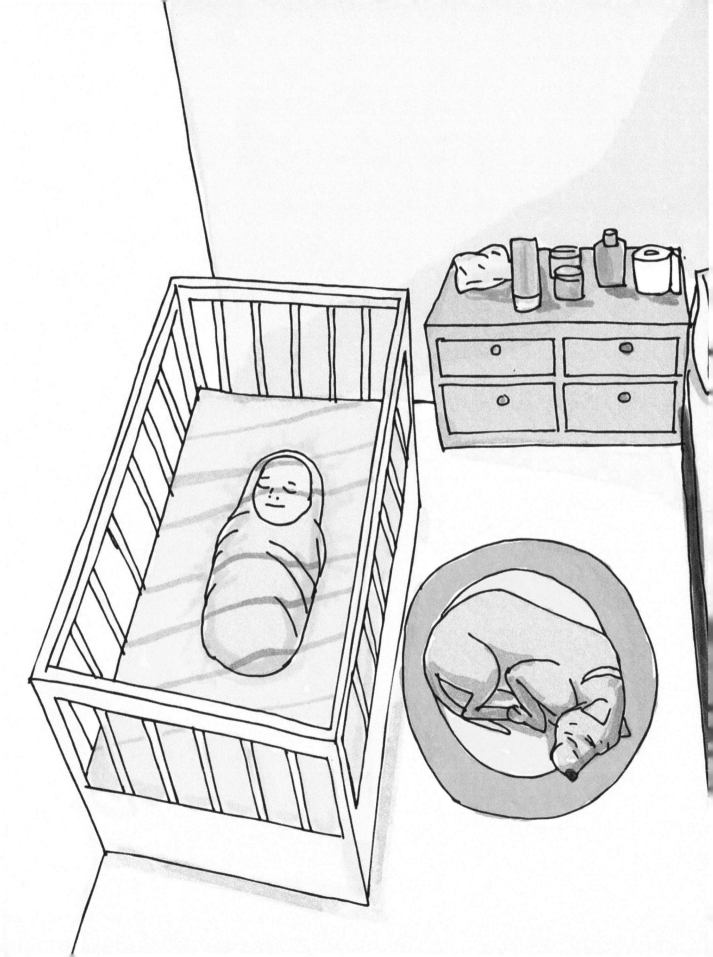

We would never hurt our baby
We would never even try

Our breed is bullied everyday
And we just don't know why

Our family is what we value most
With loyalty to show

Protect and love is what we'll do
And watch our baby grow

CPSIA information can be obtained
at www.ICGtesting.com
Printed in the USA
BVHW020006130920
588701BV00018B/536